To Annie   2006

Merry Christmas!
Love, Nana
and
Pop-Pop

D1373542

Copyright © 2001 by Nord-Süd Verlag AG, Gossau Zürich, Switzerland
First published in Switzerland under the title *Nele & Wuschel*
English translation copyright © 2001 by North-South Books Inc.

First published in the United States, Great Britain, Canada,
Australia, and New Zealand in 2001 by North-South Books,
an imprint of Nord-Süd Verlag AG, Gossau Zürich, Switzerland

Distributed in the United States by North-South Books Inc., New York

Library of Congress Cataloging-in-Publication Data is available.
The CIP catalogue record for this book is available from The British Library.

ISBN 0-7358-1424-4 (trade binding)
1 3 5 7 9 TB 10 8 6 4 2
ISBN 0-7358-1425-2 (library binding)
1 3 5 7 9 LB 10 8 6 4 2
Printed in Germany

For more information about our books, and the authors and artists
who create them, visit our web site: www.northsouth.com

Anne Liersch

Nell & Fluffy

Illustrated by Christa Unzner

Translated by J. Alison James

North-South Books
New York · London

Nell loved animals—even bugs and spiders and snakes. She had a walrus chair, a pair of tiger slippers and all kinds of toy animals. The only thing she was missing was an animal that was actually alive.

On her sixth birthday Nell found a small cardboard box on the birthday table. It had holes poked in the top. Inside the box was a brown and black ball of fur. It stirred, poked out a nose, and made a quiet squeaking noise.

It was a guinea pig! Nell carefully picked him up and hugged him. "I love you already," she said. "I will take good care of you every day. I'll name you Fluffy."

The little guinea pig got a cage with straw bedding, a water bottle, and food nuggets. Every day Nell gave him a fresh carrot because he loved them so much.

He was allowed to run around the kitchen, and sometimes, when nobody was looking, he roamed down the hall to Nell's room. He liked to sniff her toys, but sometimes he thought they were food and chewed on them. Nell loved Fluffy. When she came home, she would hold him in her lap and tell him everything she'd done that day. Fluffy looked right at her and wiggled his nose, as if he understood everything.

Many months later, right before
her seventh birthday, Nell started at
the big school. She bragged to some
of the other children how wonderful
Fluffy was.

"Guinea pigs are boring," said one boy.
"They are for babies!"

A girl boasted about her golden
retriever. She said she even got to take
the dog for walks all by herself.

Nell was very upset. She didn't want a pet for babies. After all, she was in the big school now. That afternoon Fluffy didn't sit on her lap. That night in bed Nell dreamed of dogs and cats and great big horses. She had to have a bigger animal, but how could she make her parents understand? They would say she already had a pet. There was only one solution: Fluffy had to go. But where?

The next morning Nell had an idea.
She took a box, filled it with straw
and three carrots, and put Fluffy in.
On the way to school she left him
in the bushes near the entrance to
the corner shop.

"Good-bye, Fluffy," she whispered.
Her throat felt tight; and she almost
changed her mind, but then she ran
away fast.

It was a cool morning, and the little
guinea pig was used to a warm house.
He crawled out of the box, afraid
and shivering with cold. Suddenly
a horrifying, huge animal lunged
towards him, barking wildly.

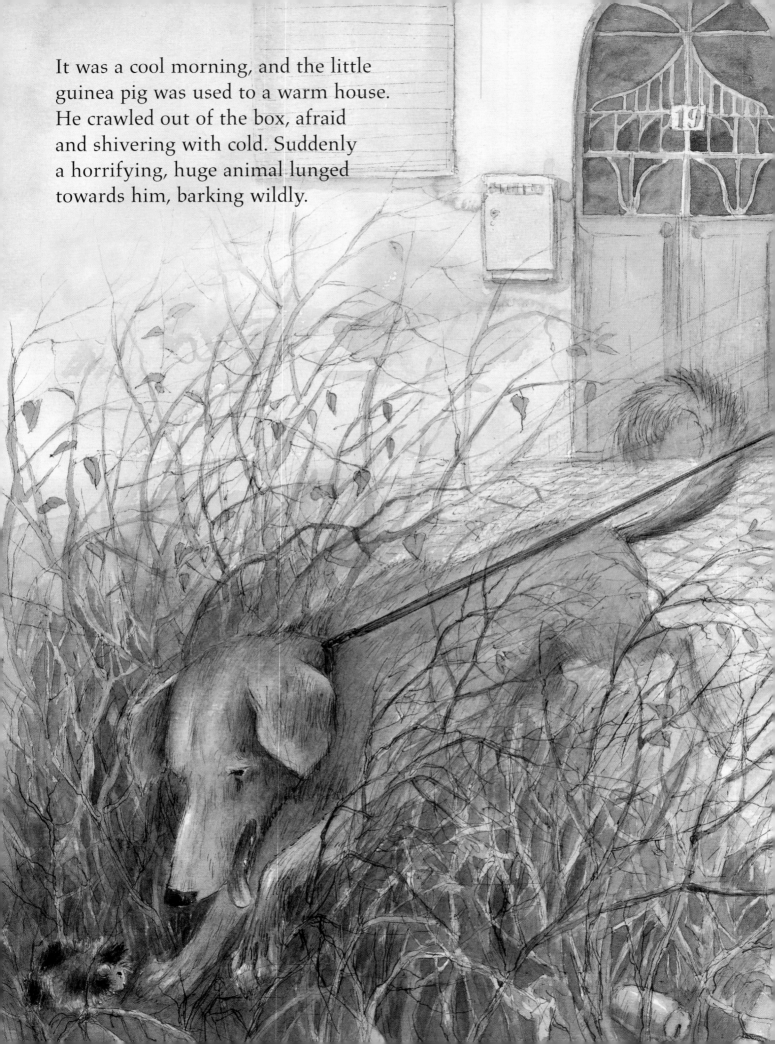

"What is it, Lottie?" asked an old woman. Then she saw the ball of fur in the bushes. She picked him up and stroked his damp hair. "For goodness' sake, look at that. An abandoned guinea pig! We'd better take the poor fellow with us, or he'll freeze in the night."
Quietly the dog nudged Fluffy, and barked a short, happy bark. Then the three of them went home.

That afternoon Nell told her parents.
"I gave Fluffy away," she declared.
"Guinea pigs are only for little babies.
Next week is my birthday and I want
a cat, or even better, a dog."
"Where is Fluffy now?" asked her father.
"I can't tell you," Nell said, looking at
the floor.
Her father was angry. "You have a pet
that you are responsible for," he said
in a stern voice, and he sent her to her
room until she would say where she
had taken Fluffy.

It was awful in her room. She was deeply ashamed of what she'd done, and she missed Fluffy. She longed to hold something warm and soft and tell him her problems, but he was outside alone in a box.

Finally Nell couldn't stand it any longer. She put on her jacket and ran to the shop on the corner. But in the bushes there was only the empty box.

"Fluffy, it's me! Come here, please!"
cried Nell. But he was gone. Then she
started to cry. She was sobbing hard
by the time she got home. Her parents
listened to what she had to say. They
did not comfort her like they always
did when she was upset. They were
still very angry with her.
"I'm sorry!" she cried. "I'm so sorry.
What can I do? I want him back!"

Nell sat in her room after she was supposed to be asleep and drew pictures of Fluffy. In the morning she asked her parents to help make some signs. They weren't angry anymore, and they wrote the notice: *Lost, brown and black guinea pig. Reward for finding him.*

For three days Nell hoped and waited. She ate almost nothing and looked pale and ill.

The fourth day was her birthday.
Nell sat with her parents at the
birthday table. Before her lay
wonderful presents, and her mother
had made a delicious birthday cake.
But Nell didn't touch a thing.
Suddenly the doorbell rang.

At the door stood an old woman with a dog and a basket covered with a cloth. "Happy birthday," said the woman. The dog sniffed at Nell and wagged his tail. "I know I asked for a dog," Nell said. "And thank you very much, but I don't want one anymore."

"Did you hear that, Lottie? She doesn't want you," the old woman said to her dog. "But perhaps she'll want to take a look in my basket to see what's inside?" Nell both laughed and cried for joy when she found Fluffy in the basket. Then she ran to her parents. She had to get the money for the reward.

"I don't need any reward," the woman said. "I spoke with your parents earlier. We decided that instead of money, you could help me. I have a hard time taking Lottie out often enough. Your parents said you can walk Lottie every day. You just have to promise not to leave her alone somewhere!"

Nell smiled a huge smile and promised to be responsible.

As Nell lay in bed that evening, Fluffy sat next to her in the box and squeaked quietly about how afraid he'd been, and how he'd longed to come back home. Nell promised never to leave him again, and then she happily fell asleep.